THE LUCKY EASTER HAT

By Joanne Mattern and Erica David
Illustrated by Jay Johnson

ISBN 0-439-80902-9
© 2006 Scholastic Entertainment Inc. All rights reserved.
SCHOLASTIC, MAYA & MIGUEL, and logos are trademarks of Scholastic Inc.
All Rights Reserved.
Published by Scholastic Inc. SCHOLASTIC and associated logos
are trademarks and/or registered trademarks of Scholastic Inc.

12 11 10 9 8 7 6 5 4 3 2 1   6 7 8 9 10/0

Printed in the U.S.A.
First printing, February 2006

SCHOLASTIC INC.

New York   Toronto   London   Auckland   Sydney
Mexico City   New Delhi   Hong Kong   Buenos Aires

It was the day before the Community Center
Easter egg hunt.

Maya was looking for the egg-decorating kit in
Abuela's trunk.

"What's this?" Maya asked.
"That is a special Easter hat," Abuela said.
"It always brought me luck."

"May I wear it?" Maya asked.
"Of course," Abuela answered. "I wore it when
I was your age."

Maya went downstairs.
"Look at my new Easter hat!" she said to Miguel.

Miguel laughed. "That's some hat!"
"Don't laugh, Miguel. Abuela says it's lucky," Maya explained.

"There's no such thing as a lucky hat," said Miguel.
"You'll see," Maya replied.

Abuela came downstairs.
"Have you two found the Easter egg paints?" she asked.

"No, not yet," Maya responded.
"Where could they be?" said Miguel.

The twins looked all over the house.
Finally, Maya found the paints in the sofa.

"Here they are!" said Maya.
"But I looked there already!" Miguel exclaimed.

"Yes, but you weren't wearing the lucky hat,"
Maya answered.

The twins sat down to decorate their eggs.
They worked and worked.

After a while Maya's basket was full.
Miguel looked up in surprise. He had only painted four eggs.

"How did you do that?" Miguel asked.
"Just lucky, I guess," Maya replied.
"There is no such thing as a lucky hat!"
Miguel shouted.

"You'll see," Maya said calmly.

The next morning, the Santos family
walked to the Community Center.

Maya and Miguel brought their eggs for the Easter egg hunt.

Once the eggs were hidden, the hunt began.

"Let's team up, Maya," Miguel suggested. "Together we'll find more eggs."

"No thanks," Maya said. "All I need is my hat to win."

Everyone rushed to find as many eggs as they could.

But Maya took her time. She knew that Abuela's lucky hat had the power to help her win.

Finally, the hunt was over.
The eggs were counted to see who had won.

They were about to announce the winner.
Maya was sure that she had won. She stepped
forward to receive the prize.

"And the winner is . . . Miguel Santos!"
Mr. Nelson announced.
Miguel was delighted.

"But my lucky hat!" Maya cried.
"I was supposed to win!"

"Maya, the hat isn't magic. It can't make you win,"
Abuela explained. "Only you can do that."

"So it hasn't brought me luck?"
Maya asked, disappointed.

"I wouldn't say that," Abuela answered.
"Look at your wonderful family and friends."
"You're a very lucky girl," she told Maya.

"See?" Maya said, turning to Miguel.

"I guess you were right," he admitted. "There is such a thing as a lucky hat."